By Olivia Abtahi, M.A.Sc.
Illustrated by Mike Love

## Publishing Credits

Rachelle Cracchiolo, M.S.Ed., *Publisher*
Conni Medina, M.A.Ed., *Editor in Chief*
Nika Fabienke, Ed.D., *Content Director*
Véronique Bos, *Creative Director*
Shaun N. Bernadou, *Art Director*
Noelle Cristea, M.A.Ed., *Senior Editor*
John Leach, *Assistant Editor*
Jess Johnson, *Graphic Designer*

## Image Credits

Illustrated by Mike Love

## Library of Congress Cataloging-in-Publication Data

Names: Abtahi, Olivia, author. | Love, Mike (Illustrator), illustrator.
Title: Secrets aboard the Barnard Star / by Olivia Abtahi ; illustrated by
    Mike Love.
Description: Huntington Beach, CA : Teacher Created Materials, [2020] |
    Includes book club questions. | Audience: Age 10. | Audience: Grades
    4-6.
Identifiers: LCCN 2019029966 (print) | LCCN 2019029967 (ebook) | ISBN
    9781644913642 (paperback) | ISBN 9781644914540 (ebook)
Subjects: LCSH: Readers (Elementary) | Space ships--Juvenile fiction.
Classification: LCC PE1119 .A25 2020  (print) | LCC PE1119  (ebook) | DDC
    428.6/2--dc23
LC record available at https://lccn.loc.gov/2019029966
LC ebook record available at https://lccn.loc.gov/2019029967

5301 Oceanus Drive
Huntington Beach, CA 92649-1030
www.tcmpub.com

## ISBN 978-1-6449-1364-2

© 2020 Teacher Created Materials, Inc.
Printed in China
Nordica.082019.CA21901551

# Table of Contents

4

CHAPTER ONE

⚛

# Welcome to the
# *Barnard Star*

Sohrab and Bruno didn't live in
a house, or an apartment, or a cabin
somewhere in the woods.  They lived on
the *Barnard Star*, a spaceship named
after the sun at center of what would
soon be their new solar system.

Both boys were born on the spaceship, and so were their parents. They had only known a life in space.

All their grandparents had been born in Earth's gravity. Bruno's told him mouthwatering stories of delicious foods like *asados*, *mollejas*, and *empanadas*. Sohrab's grandparents spoke in a mix of Persian and English, describing the beautifully woven rugs, the expertly written calligraphy, and the famous poets of Iran. They all liked to tell the boys about how, on Earth, the sky was so blue and the grass was so green that it looked different from the endless black night sprinkled with stars outside their spaceship.

According to Bruno's grandparents, they grew up in a country called Argentina. As fascinating as pictures and stories of Earth were, Bruno's favorite activity was learning more about their new home, Ophiuchus, the planet that circled Barnard's star. *Ophiuchus* was kind of a mouthful though, so everyone on the ship just called it Ophi. Bruno would stare at photos of Ophi for hours, looking at the icy veins of the planet, which held water, and the rocky surface that looked more like Mars than Earth. He couldn't wait to land.

Sohrab, on the other hand, loved living aboard the *Barnard*, where he could watch people in close quarters and observe their habits.

Why did he love people watching? Because Sohrab loved solving mysteries, and humans were more mysterious than any planet would ever be.

Almost a thousand people lived on their ship, and it was one of hundreds that had left Earth almost 40 years ago. People from countries all over Earth had boarded different spaceships. Everyone was headed to planets near different suns with names like Proxima Centauri, TRAPPIST-1, and Kepler. People didn't really come from countries anymore—they came from spaceships.

If you asked Sohrab, life aboard the spaceship was way more fun than life on a planet. With so many people aboard the *Barnard*, he had a lot of opportunities to watch everyone, learn from them, find out what they were hiding, and (more importantly) find out why they were hiding it.

Every morning, the entire ship met in the auditorium to go over daily announcements. They announced things like the menu of the mess hall, maintenance updates, and volunteer opportunities to help in the greenhouse or the school. On a Monday morning that seemed like any other, Bruno was half-listening to the announcements. His mind began drifting when the captain ended the announcements with a warning.

They had never heard a warning before.

CHAPTER TWO

# The Water Thief

"There have been several thefts of water credits lately," the captain began. "Whoever is stealing water from other passengers, please stop. Stealing water is a serious crime aboard the *Barnard*, and rest assured, we will get to the bottom of this."

The whole room filled with whispers. Who would steal *water credits*? Water was very scarce on a spaceship, and every milliliter had to be accounted for. To steal someone's water credits meant you were stealing water from someone's shower or their morning teeth cleaning. *Nobody* had ever stolen a water credit before.

Sohrab turned to Bruno. Bruno groaned. He knew what was coming.

"Bruno, I believe we have a mystery on our hands."

"Not again," Bruno sighed. He had learned an expression from his grandpa: *estar remando en dulce de leche*. He had neither rowed nor tasted the sweetness of *dulce de leche*, but he knew what his grandpa meant. Every time he went along with one of Sohrab's ideas, he ended up in a sticky situation, trying to row his way out of it.

Last week, Sohrab had insisted on finding out why the carrots in the greenhouse had turned blue. It turned out the soil had simply gone acidic after too much exposure to radiation. But Sohrab had still shouted "AHA!" at the master gardener when he heard this.

"Maybe we could just let the captain find out who stole the water. They're already working on it," Bruno pleaded.

Sohrab shook his head. "No chance. This case has our names written all over it, waiting to be solved."

"It does?"

Sohrab quickly scribbled on the notebook he carried around with him and showed Bruno a page. It read, "Sohrab and Bruno's Case of the Missing Water Credits."

"It does," Sohrab said, handing Bruno the notebook.

That afternoon after school, Sohrab led Bruno to the maintenance sector. That was where access to the pipes and valves that supplied oxygen and water throughout the ship was housed. It was one of the areas where the gravity was stronger than in the rest of the ship.

Bruno felt his feet get heavier as soon as Sohrab ushered them through the gravity lock.

"I hate this gravity. It makes me feel heavy and slow," Bruno said.

Sohrab nodded. "It's supposed to replicate the gravity on Ophi, so it's stronger than Earth's. Come on!"

Sohrab quickly hacked into the ship's water logs on a touch screen.

"Should we be doing this? What if we get caught?"

"See? You can see how many water rations every family gets," Sohrab pointed to the chart, ignoring Bruno's question. "Here."

Bruno sighed and looked closely at the water logs. He noticed that some families had significantly less water credits than other families. Sohrab's family was given 70 water credits a week, while Bruno's family received 56. Some families only got 35.

"How come some families only get 35 water credits a week?" Bruno asked.

That was basically just enough for one person to shower three times a week or have eight glasses of water a day.

Sohrab frowned. "I think we get more credits because my parents are scientists and yours are doctors."

Bruno still wondered why other families got less. Just because they had a different job didn't mean they were less thirsty. Humans were humans. They all needed water.

Sohrab stared at the touch screen, deep in thought. The sounds of heavy footsteps echoed from the back of the maintenance sector. Someone was coming. Sohrab was glad for the stronger gravity here. Otherwise, they wouldn't be able to hear someone coming until it was too late.

"Are we allowed to be here?" Bruno whispered.

"No," Sohrab said. And they hurried out of the room before anyone saw.

# CHAPTER THREE

# Another Mystery

The next day, Bruno had to volunteer in the ship's clinic, while Sohrab was helping his parents over in the science wing. Every kid aboard the *Barnard* was required to have an apprenticeship. Bruno had decided to apprentice as a doctor, just like his parents had.

Today, he was helping treat Eric, a boy a year ahead of him in school. Eric had some nasty cuts on his arm. Bruno had never seen an infection before because the ship was so sterile—but he recognized it from pictures.

"How did you hurt your arm like that?" Bruno asked as he applied antiseptic to the cuts. Eric winced.

"My arm got jammed in a trash chute," Eric explained.

Bruno didn't say anything. The trash chutes opened and closed so fast before ejecting waste into space that it would be easy to get caught in the doors. But the patterns of Eric's cuts didn't match the clean, smooth lines of the trash chute doors.

Also, how could a cut from a trash chute give him such a bad infection? Everything on the ship was clean because it was so hard for bacteria to live in the ship's environment. Even the yogurt they made on board was tough to culture.

Bruno put antibacterial ointment onto Eric's arm and wrapped it in gauze, finishing up.

Before Eric walked out the door, Bruno called out, "Just don't wash it tonight, OK? It's important that the ointment stay on overnight."

Eric laughed. "Like I have enough water credits to even clean up properly."

And with that, Eric left.

While Bruno was in the ship's clinic, Sohrab was working with his parents on a geological survey. This week, they'd been testing rock samples from planet Ophiuchus. Over 60 years ago, a robot had been sent to Ophi. The robot collected samples and got readings of the planet to test whether humans could survive there.

Sohrab put a slide under his microscope. But today, he was doing a different experiment today.

"Mom?" he called out. "I need two hydrogen atoms and one oxygen atom, please."

His mom laughed. "Are you trying to make water?"

Sohrab nodded his head, frowning. Why was his mother laughing?

"Sohrab," she said, sitting down next to him, "you can't just make $H_2O$ by mashing hydrogen and oxygen together. If we could, then we wouldn't have left Earth in the first place."

Sohrab took a deep breath, his heart sinking. He'd thought that if he could make water, he could solve the issue of people needing to steal it.

"So how do we have enough water to live on board if we can't make it?"

Sohrab's mother sat down, taking off her glasses. "When we left Earth, we made sure we had enough water to last us 80 years. That means every spill, every drop, every molecule of $H_2O$ has to be accounted for. There's a set amount of water on the ship, Sohrab-joon."

Sohrab knew that when his mother used the affectionate word *joon* after his name, she was trying to soften the blow of whatever she was going to say next.

"We recycle everything we can so that we have some cushion if we can't find water on the planet right away. That's why stealing water rations is so bad."

Sohrab nodded, finally understanding how serious it was to steal water. They weren't just stealing water from everyone on the ship. They were stealing water from future generations on the *Barnard*.

"Who would steal water, then?"

"All living things need water, Sohrab. Whoever stole it must need it very badly," his mother replied.

CHAPTER FOUR

☙

# Not All Fun and Games

One of the best parts of growing up on a ship was the gravity-free games. Instead of using a ball, the way kids played on Earth, the *children* were the balls. The object of the game spaceball was for someone from your team to enter the opposite goal. The only catch was you had to tag at least two teammates before you attempted to score a goal.

Eric floated near the far goal, holding his arm close to his chest.

"What's wrong with Eric's arm?" Sohrab wondered out loud.

"Oh, he cut his arm.  It was infected. I'd never seen an infection before," Bruno said under his breath.

Sohrab frowned.  For once, Bruno frowned too.

The two teams floated in the gym, waiting for the whistle.  The second it blew, Sohrab propelled himself toward Bruno and tagged him.  From there, Bruno pushed off a wall to tag Maria, who was closest to the other team's goal. Since their team had tagged twice, Sohrab gave Maria a light shove that pushed her into the opposite goal.

While this was going on, their teammates Krishna and Jinhua shot backward to defend their goal against Eric, who was being pushed by Joe to score for the opposing team.

"No!" Eric yelled at Joe. "I don't want to score! Don't touch me!"

Krishna and Jinhua shrugged, then linked arms to block Eric's path.

"OW!" Eric cried, as he crashed into the girls' arms. He pushed off a wall and glided out of the gym, tears floating behind him.

"Eric!" Sohrab shouted. "Wait up!"

He and Eric had never really been that close, but he knew deep down that something wasn't right. He had an idea about what had actually hurt Eric's arm.

Sohrab saw a door close around a bend in the hallway. He walked toward it and knocked. Nobody answered. Maybe he was wrong and hadn't followed Eric to the right quarters. He waited a moment, and just as he was turning to leave, he heard a voice on the other side let out a sharp cry of pain.

"Eric?" Sohrab raised his voice and called out. "I know you're in there. Are you OK? I just want to help."

Sohrab heard muffled crying on the other side of the door. He knocked again, this time softer, noticing that his first knock had pushed the door slightly ajar. He knew that going in without permission was against the ship's rules, but he gave the door a push and stepped inside.

And there, in the middle of the room, floated a big sphere of water.

# CHAPTER FIVE

❁

# The Stowaway

Sohrab had never seen so much water before. Sure, he had seen images of Earth, but never had he seen water like that in real life. Eric had turned the gravity off in his quarters to store it all in one giant ball.

"You shouldn't be in here!" Eric said, suddenly appearing from his bedroom.

Pulled from his thoughts, Sohrab turned on the magnets in his shoes so that he would stop floating. He turned to Eric.

"Where is it?" he asked calmly. "Where's the thing that hurt you?"

Eric looked pale as he zoomed past Sohrab and closed the front door. He was obviously very upset and kept looking around.

"I can help you, Eric." He wished Bruno were there. Bruno would know how to calm Eric down. Sohrab began to get out his communication tablet to call him.

"No!" Eric shouted. His panic was evident as his voice rose. He squeaked out, "You can't tell anyone!"

Sohrab put down the tablet. "I won't." He lowered his voice, trying to calm him down. "I want to help. Just show me the animal that bit you."

And just then, as if on cue, a turtle floated into the room.

In the end, Sohrab convinced Eric to
let Bruno come over.  Bruno watched,
amazed, as the turtle floated through
the room.  It skimmed into the sphere
of water and out again.  There were
no animals on the *Barnard*, so the
boys were fascinated by the creature
and momentarily forgot about the
stolen water.

"But where did you get a turtle?" Bruno asked, stunned. Eric reached out to caress the turtle's shell as it floated past him.

"Your grandparents must have brought him on board when he was just a baby," Sohrab said. "But they didn't count on him living this long. And when he started to look sick, you thought you could help him with water. But it wasn't easy, was it? He bit you, even when you were trying to help."

Eric sighed. "Yeah. Mickey hasn't been feeling well lately."

"So you thought letting him swim would help," Sohrab said, gesturing to the floating water ball. "That's why you stole water from the ship."

Eric looked down. "I didn't know what else to do. And now I'll get in trouble."

Sohrab frowned. He had on his thinking face. "I have an idea."

Bruno sighed. He usually hated when Sohrab said that.

# CHAPTER SIX

ॐ

# The Ship's New Mascot

Sohrab got permission from the captain to make an announcement during the morning assembly.

"Hello everyone," Sohrab waved. His voice was clear, and he wasn't afraid to be talking to a thousand people. His grandmother had given him courage by reminding him that he was named after a legendary warrior from a famous poem. He knew it would sound silly to say aloud that he felt like a warrior, but he was proud of his ability to uncover the truth and help Eric too.

"We have solved the mystery of the missing water credits!" Sohrab happily announced. At that moment, Bruno unveiled the glass box next to him. Inside was Mickey, chewing happily on a piece of lettuce.

The entire crew of the ship gasped.

"As you can see, Mickey is a turtle. He's about 40 years old. We estimate he has another 40 years to go. Turtles enjoy swimming every now and then. Eric here was simply trying to make sure Mickey was comfortable," Sohrab said, nodding to Eric who was also standing on the stage. "That's why he took more water than he was allowed."

"Now, we know water credits are precious. But if the ship agrees, we would like to let Mickey enjoy water whenever he can. It would be nice to have a ship mascot, especially since we have no other pets.

"If everyone donates just a bit of their water rations, Mickey can swim in gravity by the maintenance sector."

Sohrab looked expectantly at Bruno, who took a deep breath to calm himself. "We would like to vote on whether everyone aboard is willing to give up some water. All those in favor?" Bruno's voice was shaky.

Sohrab and Eric raised their hands. Slowly, they watched as others lifted their hands in agreement. Not everyone raised a hand. But when the captain raised his, it became almost unanimous.

"It's settled then!" Sohrab shouted. "Mickey will become our ship's mascot!"

Eric beamed. He took Mickey out of the tank and held him up for everyone to see. The entire ship clapped.

The case of the missing water credits had been solved, *and* the ship got a new mascot!

# About Us

## The Author
Olivia Abtahi is a children's literature writer and commercial video director. Her debut novel, *Twin Flames*, won the 2018 New Visions Award. She received a BFA in film and television and a master's in advertising. She lives in Denver, Colorado, with her husband and cat.

## The Illustrator
From astronauts and knights to vampires and dragons, Mike Love has a love for working with imagination and narrative! His projects range from traditional children's books and educational publications to graphic novels and sticker books. He has a master's degree in fine art and loves to return to his university each year to check out up-and-coming illustrators.